The
Goa Trip

A Journey Beyond Reality

A thrilling adventure of six friends who set out for a fun trip to Goa, only to find themselves entangled in a web of mystery, suspense, and the supernatural.

By

Ajay Chavan

Copyright Page

The Goa Trip: A Journey Beyond Reality

Published by Notion Press Chennai, India

www.notionpress.com

Dedication

To all the friends who turn ordinary trips into unforgettable adventures.

And to those who dare to explore the unknown may you always find the thrill in the journey.

Preface

What was supposed to be an exciting getaway to Goa turned into a mind-bending journey beyond reality. This story follows six friends Ajay, Saket, Nikhil, Ganesh, Om and Aryan who set out for a fun filled trip, only to find themselves trapped in an eerie and mysterious chain of events.

With every step, the line between illusion and truth blurs, friendships are tested, and a hidden force lurking in the shadows threatens their very existence. Adventure, comedy, thrill, and suspense blend together as the group uncovers the shocking truth behind their journey.

This book is for those who crave adventure, cherish friendship, and love a good mystery with a twist of humor. Get ready to experience

"The Goa Trip: A Journey Beyond Reality."

Ajay Chavan

CONTENT

CONTENT

Chapter 1: The Goa Dream

Ajay, Saket, Nikhil, Ganesh, Om, and Aryan sat in their favorite roadside café, sipping chai and munching on samosas. It was a typical evening casual banter, exaggerated stories, and Saket's usual overexcited ideas. But tonight, the conversation took an unexpected turn.

"Guys, we've been talking about this Goa trip for years. It's time to make it happen!" Saket declared, slamming his hand on the table dramatically, causing a few heads to turn their way.

Om, ever the mature one, raised an eyebrow. "And what makes you think it'll actually happen this time? We've planned this trip at least five times, and every single time, something went wrong. Remember last time? Nikhil had food poisoning, Aryan's parents refused to let him go, and Ajay "

" was too busy eating to even care," Nikhil finished, shaking his head. "Classic."

Ajay, who had been busy stuffing his face with samosas, finally looked up. "Yeah, yeah, sounds great. But more importantly, does Goa have good food? Because if I'm spending money on this trip, I better get the best seafood thali ever."

Saket groaned. "Bro, Goa is famous for its food! You can eat all you want, but let's focus on getting there first."

Nikhil, the travel enthusiast, was already pulling up lists on his phone. "Okay, so there are a few ways we can do this. Flight, train, or the best option ROAD TRIP!"

Aryan immediately choked on his chai. "Road trip? Are you guys crazy? That's like… 12-14 hours of non stop travel! And what if we get lost? What if the car breaks down in the middle of nowhere? What if "

" we actually have an amazing adventure?" Om interrupted with a smirk. "Relax, Aryan. A road trip will be fun. We'll make stops, enjoy the ride, and experience the real thrill of the journey."

Ganesh, the business minded one, leaned forward. "Forget the ride. Do you know how many tourists visit Goa? We can make some serious money. Maybe open a temporary business there rent out bikes, sell custom t shirts. It's a gold mine!"

Saket clapped. "Now that's the spirit, Ganesh! Always thinking ahead. Maybe we can even start a beachside food stall and let Ajay be the official taste tester."

Ajay grinned. "Now that's a business idea I can get behind."

Om sighed, running a hand through his hair. "Alright, jokes aside, let's be real. We need to plan this properly. Who's handling what?"

Nikhil raised his hand. "I'll take care of the itinerary places to visit, food spots, hidden gems, everything."

Ganesh nodded. "I'll figure out the expenses and see if we can cut costs anywhere."

Ajay yawned. "I'll handle the snacks."

Aryan, looking skeptical but knowing he had no choice, muttered, "I'll bring the first aid kit… and probably a list of emergency contacts."

Saket was practically bouncing in his seat. "And I'll handle the fun! Pranks, games, and everything else to make this trip legendary!"

By the end of the evening, the plan was set. A road trip to Goa, one car, six friends, and an adventure waiting to unfold.

As they walked out of the café, the excitement buzzed in the air. Saket was already imagining beach parties, Nikhil dreamed of scenic sunsets, Ganesh calculated the best ways to make a quick buck, Aryan mentally prepared for disasters, Om stayed grounded in reality, and Ajay? Well, he was still thinking about food.

Little did they know, this trip would be nothing like they had imagined. Between mystery, thrill, and sheer madness, their Goa trip would become the most unforgettable chapter of their lives.

Chapter 2: The Road Trip Begins

The day had finally arrived. The bags were packed, the car was fueled up, and six excited yet chaotic friends were ready to hit the road. Or at least, that's what they thought.

"Where is Ajay?" Om asked, rubbing his temples. It was 6 AM, and the plan was to leave early to avoid traffic. But, as expected, Ajay was missing.

"Probably eating breakfast," Nikhil said, rolling his eyes.

As if on cue, Ajay appeared with a bag of parathas. "Guys, we need to eat well before a long journey. You don't want me getting cranky halfway through."

Aryan looked at him in disbelief. "We are supposed to leave at six! It's already past six thirty! We're going to be late!"

Saket, always high on energy, jumped into the driver's seat. "Relax, Aryan! The real fun begins now!"

With everyone finally seated, bags stuffed in the trunk, and music blasting through the speakers, the journey to Goa began. The first few hours were filled with laughter, arguments over music choices, and Saket's overenthusiastic driving that made Aryan grip his seat in fear.

Halfway through the journey, they stopped at a roadside dhaba for lunch. "Best part of road trips? These dhabas," Ajay said, as he ordered a massive plate of butter chicken.

Ganesh, meanwhile, was calculating their expenses. "We need to be smart with our money. No unnecessary spending."

"Too late," Aryan said, pointing to Saket, who was busy buying a bunch of random souvenirs from a street vendor.

Just as they were about to leave, a mysterious old man approached them. "Going to Goa, are you?" he asked in a raspy voice.

The group exchanged glances. "Uh… yeah?" Om replied cautiously.

The old man nodded. "Beware of the road ahead. Strange things happen on this highway at night."

Aryan's face paled. "What kind of things?"

The old man chuckled. "Let's just say… some travelers never reach their destination."

The group laughed it off, assuming it was just another roadside storyteller trying to spook them. But as they drove away, a strange feeling settled in.

A few hours later, the sun began to set, casting an orange glow over the highway. The mood inside the car had shifted slightly Saket was still excited, but the others had started to feel the fatigue of the journey. Even Nikhil, the travel enthusiast, had stopped chatting and was quietly gazing out the window.

Om stretched in his seat. "How much longer, Nikhil?"

Nikhil checked his phone. "Still about five hours. But we need to be careful. The next stretch of road is known to be a bit… tricky."

Aryan sat up straight. "What do you mean by tricky?"

"Just that the road is poorly lit, and there have been stories about weird things happening here at night," Nikhil said casually.

Aryan gulped. "You mean, like what that old man said?"

Ajay, completely unfazed, yawned. "Guys, please, it's just a road. The only weird thing that can happen is running out of food, and that, my friends, is a true horror story."

Saket laughed. "Exactly! Stop worrying, Aryan. We've got a long way to go, and I'm sure nothing creepy is going to happen."

At that moment, the car suddenly jerked. The engine sputtered, and Saket struggled to keep control of the wheel as the vehicle started slowing down.

"Uh… guys?" Saket said, gripping the steering wheel tightly. "I think we have a problem."

The car came to a halt in the middle of the highway. The surroundings were eerily silent, with no other vehicles in sight. They were surrounded by dense trees on either side of the road, their branches swaying slightly in the evening breeze.

Ganesh frowned. "What happened?"

Saket turned the key again, but the car refused to start. "I don't know. It was running fine just a second ago."

Aryan's breathing quickened. "Okay, okay, this is bad. We're stuck. In the middle of nowhere. At night. And an old man literally warned us about this!"

Om, always the rational one, got out of the car and popped the hood. "Let's check the engine."

Nikhil and Ganesh followed him, while Aryan hesitated before stepping out cautiously. The air around them felt heavy, almost unnatural. It was as if something was watching them from the shadows.

Ajay, still sitting inside the car, shouted, "You guys figure it out. I'll guard the snacks."

Saket tried to lighten the mood. "Oh, great, Ajay. Thanks for your valuable contribution."

But just then, a sudden rustling noise came from the nearby trees. Everyone froze.

"What… was that?" Aryan whispered, his voice barely audible.

The rustling stopped. The night grew even quieter, almost as if the forest itself was holding its breath.

Om slowly turned back toward the car. "Let's not panic. Let's just fix the car and "

Before he could finish, the car's headlights flickered on by themselves.

The group exchanged nervous glances.

Something was definitely not right.

Chapter 3: The Haunted Highway

The car's headlights flickered eerily, casting dancing shadows on the empty highway. The group stood frozen, their breaths caught in their throats. Aryan, who was already on edge, nearly jumped out of his skin.

"What the hell was that?" he whispered.

Om, ever the rational one, tried to find an explanation. "Maybe it's just a wiring issue." He moved cautiously toward the driver's seat to check the dashboard.

"But the engine wasn't starting," Ganesh pointed out. "How did the lights turn on by themselves?"

Nikhil peered into the darkness beyond the car. The highway was surrounded by dense trees, their twisted branches swaying in the wind like eerie hands reaching out. A chill ran down his spine. "Guys… I don't like this place."

Saket, ever the fearless one, clapped his hands. "Come on, you all are overthinking! Maybe it's a loose connection, or maybe the car just needed a moment. Let's try to start it again."

He hopped into the driver's seat and turned the key. The engine roared to life as if nothing had happened. Everyone exhaled in relief.

"See? Nothing to worry about," Saket said triumphantly. "Now let's get moving before Aryan has a heart attack."

As they all piled back into the car, Ajay reached for a bag of chips. "Man, that was intense. I need to eat something to calm my nerves."

"Ajay, you always need to eat something," Om sighed as he fastened his seatbelt.

As Saket drove forward, the group tried to shake off the eerie feeling. But the highway felt… different. The air was heavier, and the road seemed endless, stretching far beyond what it should have. They hadn't passed another vehicle in what felt like hours.

"Are we sure we're on the right road?" Ganesh asked, checking the GPS on his phone.

"Of course, we are," Nikhil assured him. "It's a straight road to Goa."

But something was wrong.

The GPS screen glitched for a moment before the navigation app completely shut down.

"Uh, guys…?" Ganesh murmured, tapping at his phone. "I lost signal."

Everyone checked their phones, and one by one, they all realized the same thing.

"No network," Om confirmed. "That's weird."

Aryan swallowed hard. "Okay, I officially don't like this."

The road ahead seemed to stretch into infinity, with no sign of the next town, no streetlights, and no familiar landmarks. The silence was deafening.

Then, out of nowhere, the radio crackled to life.

A deep, distorted voice echoed through the speakers. "TURN BACK."

Saket slammed the brakes. The car screeched to a stop, and everyone sat in stunned silence, staring at the radio.

Aryan gripped the seat. "Tell me you all heard that."

Before anyone could answer, the voice spoke again, this time lower, almost a whisper.

"Turn back… before it's too late."

The car was filled with an eerie chill, as if an invisible presence had crept inside.

Ajay dropped his chips. "Okay. That's it. I'm out."

Nikhil shook his head, trying to stay calm. "Maybe… maybe it's a prank? Some truckers messing around with a radio frequency?"

But deep down, none of them believed that.

Ganesh, usually the most logical one, looked shaken. "What do we do?"

Silence hung in the air. No one had an answer.

Then, suddenly, they saw it.

A figure standing in the middle of the road ahead.

A woman in a white dress, her hair covering her face, standing completely still in the car's headlights.

The friends sat frozen, their minds struggling to process what they were seeing.

The woman slowly raised her hand… and pointed directly at them.

Saket gripped the steering wheel tightly, his knuckles turning white. "Guys… what do I do?"

"Drive around her, slowly," Om suggested, trying to sound calm but failing.

"No way!" Aryan exclaimed. "What if she jumps in front of the car?"

Ajay took a deep breath. "Okay. Let's think logically. Maybe she needs help?"

"HELP?!" Aryan practically screeched. "She's standing in the middle of the road like a horror movie ghost, and you think she needs help?!"

Before anyone could respond, the woman started moving. But she wasn't walking. She was gliding.

A blood curdling whisper filled the car's speakers. "You shouldn't be here…"

The group collectively screamed.

Saket slammed the car into reverse, the tires screeching as he sped backward. The woman didn't move, just continued pointing at them.

Ganesh was frantically trying to reload the GPS, but the screen remained dead. "This isn't happening… this isn't happening…"

Nikhil suddenly pointed at the rearview mirror. "Guys, we have a bigger problem."

Everyone turned. The once empty road behind them was no longer empty.

Dozens of shadowy figures had appeared, standing in eerie silence, their faces obscured by darkness. They weren't moving just standing and watching.

The air inside the car grew suffocating. Panic surged through the group as an overwhelming sense of dread took over.

Then, just as suddenly as it had started, the radio shut off. The figures vanished. The woman disappeared. The headlights illuminated nothing but an empty road ahead.

Silence.

Saket hesitated, his hands trembling on the wheel. "Did… did that just happen?"

Om exhaled shakily. "I don't know. But let's get the hell out of here."

No one argued. Saket hit the accelerator, speeding down the highway, desperate to leave whatever had just happened behind them.

As the car roared forward, Aryan muttered under his breath, "I told you guys this trip was a bad idea."

No one disagreed.

Chapter 4: The Unseen Passenger

The car sped down the highway, but the eerie silence among the friends was louder than any conversation they could have had. No one dared to speak, their minds still reeling from what had just happened. The haunting image of the woman in white and the shadowy figures lingered in their thoughts, a chilling memory that refused to fade.

Saket gripped the steering wheel so tightly that his knuckles turned white. His usual overexcited demeanor was replaced by a focused intensity. "We're not stopping until we reach the nearest town," he declared, his voice unusually firm.

Om nodded in agreement, his rational mind struggling to make sense of what they had just witnessed. "Whatever that was… we're leaving it behind. No more looking back."

Aryan, who always took tension about the smallest things, was on the verge of hyperventilating. "No network, no GPS, no signboards. What if we're stuck on a loop? What if "

"Shut up, Aryan," Nikhil snapped. "Let's just get out of here first."

Ganesh, the business minded planner of the group, checked his phone one last time. "Still no signal. But we've been driving for a while now; we should be getting close to civilization."

Ajay, munching on a protein bar, finally spoke. "You guys are stressing too much. Maybe we're just overtired, and our brains imagined stuff."

Saket rolled his eyes. "Oh yeah, Ajay, we all had the exact same hallucination? Very logical."

As they drove, the tension in the air slowly began to dissipate. The familiar sight of small roadside shops and dimly lit dhabas came into view. The relief in the car was almost tangible.

"Finally!" Nikhil exhaled. "Let's stop somewhere. I need chai."

Saket pulled into a roadside dhaba, the neon sign flickering as if it too had been through a horror movie. The group got out, stretching their stiff limbs. The air was cool, carrying the scent of freshly made parathas and sizzling pakoras. A couple of trucks were parked on the side, and a few drivers sat inside, talking in hushed tones. The eerie stillness of the night made it feel like they had stepped into a different world.

As they sat down at a wooden table, a middle aged waiter approached, wiping his hands on his apron. "Aap log Goa ja rahe ho?"

Om nodded. "Haan bhaiya. Bas raste mein ek ajeeb si cheez ho gayi…"

Before he could continue, the waiter smirked knowingly. "Highway pe kuch dekha, na?"

The group exchanged uneasy glances. "How do you know?" Aryan asked hesitantly.

The waiter pulled up a chair, leaning in conspiratorially. "Yeh road purani hai. Bahut logon ne wahan ajeeb cheezein dekhi hain. Kabhi ek aurat, kabhi kuch aur…"

Nikhil shivered. "So we weren't imagining it?"

The waiter shook his head. "Nahi beta. Aap log bach gaye. Bahut log rukh jate hain, baat karne ki koshish karte hain. Fir kabhi wapas nahi aate."

The air grew thick with unease. No one knew how to respond.

Trying to shake off the creepy conversation, they ordered tea and snacks. As they sipped their chai, the laughter and warmth of the dhaba slowly brought them back to reality. Other customers came and went, and for a brief moment, it felt like things were normal again.

But then, Ajay frowned and whispered, "Guys… we have a problem."

Everyone turned to him.

He pointed at the car.

The back door was slightly open.

As if someone… or something… had gotten in.

A cold shiver ran through them.

Saket swallowed hard. "We locked the car, right?"

No one answered.

Nikhil stood up slowly, his hands balled into fists. "Maybe the door didn't close properly?" His voice lacked confidence.

Ganesh took out his phone and turned on the flashlight. "Only one way to find out."

They approached the car cautiously, each step heavier than the last. The air around them grew colder, and the sounds of the dhaba faded into the background. As Ganesh reached out to open the door fully, a gust of wind blew past them, rattling the nearby trees.

And then… they heard it.

A faint, almost imperceptible whisper from inside the car.

"Why did you leave me behind?"

A chill ran down their spines. Aryan took a step back, his breath coming in short gasps. Om reached out and gripped Saket's shoulder, his voice barely above a whisper. "Tell me you heard that."

Nikhil's hands shook slightly as he tightened his grip on his phone. "We're checking the car. Now."

Saket, despite the fear clawing at his throat, nodded and pulled the door open in one swift motion. The flashlight beam illuminated the empty back seat. Nothing. Just their bags and some scattered wrappers from Ajay's snacks.

For a moment, there was silence. Then, just as they were about to let out a relieved sigh

A child's laughter echoed from the trunk.

The group froze. Every muscle in their bodies tensed. Nikhil slowly reached for the trunk release, his fingers trembling. He pressed it, and the trunk popped open with a soft click.

Inside, there was nothing.

Just darkness.

But the laughter still rang in their ears.

And the whisper followed: "Why did you leave me behind?"

Chapter 5: The Haunting Echo

The laughter still echoed in their ears long after they had slammed the trunk shut. The friends stood frozen, their breathing shallow, their minds racing to make sense of what had just happened. The dhaba's warm glow suddenly felt distant, like a mirage in the cold darkness of the highway.

"Okay…okay…" Aryan muttered, running a hand through his hair, "Someone explain that. Right now."

"Maybe it's some kind of audio prank?" Ajay suggested, trying to keep his voice casual. "Like…a hidden speaker in the car?"

Ganesh shot him a sharp look. "Yeah, because we totally installed ghost sound effects in our car before leaving."

Saket took a deep breath, trying to regain control. "Let's get back inside. Maybe someone at the dhaba knows more about this highway."

They hurried back to their table, their eyes darting around as if expecting to see something unnatural lurking in the shadows. The waiter who had spoken to them earlier was nowhere to be seen. Instead, an older man sat behind the counter, counting cash in an ancient looking register.

Nikhil approached him hesitantly. "Excuse me, sir…we heard something weird outside. A voice… a child laughing."

The old man stopped counting. His wrinkled hands hovered over the register as he slowly lifted his head to look at them. His eyes, dull and weary, held an emotion they couldn't quite place.

"Baccha?" he repeated softly. A long pause stretched between them before he finally spoke again. "You're not the first ones to hear it."

A shiver ran through the group.

Om, always the logical one, leaned in. "What do you mean?"

The old man sighed, wiping his hands on his faded kurta. "Years ago, there was an accident on this highway. A family mother, father, and their young son were on their way to Goa when their car crashed near the bend in the road. No one survived."

Aryan swallowed hard. "And the laughter…?"

The man looked past them, towards their car parked outside. "The child's spirit…some say he doesn't realize he's dead. He still thinks he's on a road trip. Sometimes, he tries to join travelers."

A heavy silence fell over them. The warmth of the dhaba felt even thinner now, the comforting scents of food doing little to ease their fear.

"Has…has anyone seen him?" Saket asked, his voice barely above a whisper.

The old man nodded. "A few have. A small boy, sitting quietly in the backseat of their car, smiling. But by the time they look again… he's gone."

Aryan gripped the table so tightly that his knuckles turned white. "No. No, no, no. We are not dealing with a ghost kid. Absolutely not."

"Let's just get in the car and drive," Nikhil said, standing up. "Whatever this is, we're not sticking around to find out more."

They paid quickly and rushed back to their vehicle, their eyes scanning every shadow, every corner. The car seemed the same as before doors locked, windows shut.

But as Saket slid into the driver's seat and inserted the key, his stomach dropped.

The rearview mirror reflected something that shouldn't have been there.

A tiny, dusty footprint on the backseat leather.

His hands clenched the steering wheel as his pulse roared in his ears. He didn't tell the others. He couldn't. Instead, he started the engine, pressed his foot on the accelerator, and sped off into the night, the haunted highway stretching before them.

Behind them, in the distance, the sound of a child's laughter faded into the wind.

As they drove in silence, the tension in the car was thick, unspoken fears sitting heavy between them.

The road ahead was shrouded in fog, making visibility poor. The eerie stillness of the night was interrupted only by the rhythmic thudding of the tires on the pavement.

"Are we just not going to talk about what happened back there?" Aryan finally broke the silence, his voice laced with anxiety.

Saket gripped the wheel tighter. "What do you want me to say? We heard something creepy. We saw something we can't explain. Now we move on."

"Move on?" Ajay scoffed. "Dude, we literally heard a ghost kid. That's not something you just move on from!"

Nikhil, usually the adventurous one, sat unusually quiet in the passenger seat. He stared out at the passing trees, his fingers drumming against his knee. "I just hope we didn't… I don't know… bring something with us."

A chill ran through everyone.

Ganesh, the ever rational one, shook his head. "Let's not overthink this. It's probably some weird legend that got passed down. I bet there's a logical explanation."

Om, however, wasn't so sure. He had seen Saket's expression when he got into the car. Something had shaken him. "Saket, you okay?"

Saket hesitated for a moment before answering. "Yeah. Just… let's get to the hotel."

No one argued. They all wanted to put as much distance between them and the haunted highway as possible. But as the car sped forward, an unshakable feeling settled in their chests.

They weren't alone.

As they approached the next town, a signpost appeared by the roadside. It read:

Welcome to Varca – 30 km to Goa.

Relief washed over them. They were close. Soon, this would all just be a strange story to tell over drinks.

But then, from the backseat, a small voice whispered:

"Are we there yet?"

Chapter 6: Shadows in the Hotel

The car screeched to a halt in front of their hotel, a grand but slightly aged structure with an old world charm. The neon sign flickered as if it were struggling to stay alive, casting eerie glows on the damp pavement. The boys hurriedly stepped out, exchanging glances but saying nothing about the whisper they had all just heard in the car.

A weary receptionist greeted them at the front desk, barely looking up from his register. "Welcome to Sunset Inn. Three rooms, right?" his voice was monotone, his eyes heavy with exhaustion.

"Yes, please," Saket said, handing over their IDs. "We just need some rest."

The receptionist handed them their keys with an odd look. "Room 207, 208, and 209. Just… don't go wandering around too much at night."

Aryan frowned. "Why?"

The man hesitated before giving a forced chuckle. "No reason. Just… Goa has its share of stories, you know?" He waved them off before they could ask more.

The elevator creaked as it took them to the second floor. The dimly lit hallway stretched out before them, lined with identical doors. Their footsteps echoed unnervingly, each creak of the wooden floorboards making them more anxious.

"Alright," Ganesh sighed, forcing a grin. "We are here, we are safe, and we are going to sleep this weirdness off."

They split up into their assigned rooms, Aryan and Nikhil in 207, Om and Saket in 208, and Ajay and Ganesh in 209. The exhaustion from the long journey was finally catching up to them, and despite the unease in the air, they prepared to sleep.

But sleep did not come easy.

In Room 207, Aryan kept tossing and turning. The silence of the night felt too thick, too unnatural. Then, around 2 AM, he heard it a soft knock on the door.

Knock. Knock.

He froze. Nikhil was snoring beside him, unaware. Aryan swallowed hard and slowly sat up.

Knock. Knock. Knock.

He inched towards the door and peeked through the peephole. Nothing.

But as he turned to go back to bed, the knocking resumed this time, from inside the room.

A chill ran down his spine. Slowly, he turned his head toward the closet. The door, which had been closed before, now stood slightly ajar. A deep, black void stared back at him.

A creak came from inside the closet.

Aryan's breath hitched. He reached for his phone, trying to turn on the flashlight, but his hands trembled too much. Just as he was about to wake Nikhil, the closet door moved opening an inch wider.

And then, a whisper.

"Come closer."

Meanwhile, in Room 209, Ajay and Ganesh had left the balcony door slightly open to enjoy the breeze. Ganesh was already half asleep when Ajay, who had been munching on chips, suddenly sat up.

A shadow moved past the balcony.

At first, he thought it was a reflection. But then, the door creaked, moving ever so slightly.

"Ganesh," Ajay whispered. "Wake up."

Ganesh groaned, turning to the side. "Mmmh… what now?"

Ajay didn't respond. His eyes were locked on the balcony, where the shadowy figure now stood still, just beyond the glass door.

Watching them.

The streetlights flickered, casting long, distorted silhouettes through the curtain. Ajay's breath came out in short gasps as he reached for the lamp beside his bed. He flicked it on.

The balcony was empty.

He exhaled in relief. "Must be my imagination," he muttered. But just as he turned off the lamp, a deep, guttural chuckle echoed from outside.

In Room 208, Saket and Om had the strangest experience of all. Om was a light sleeper, so when he heard the faint sound of footsteps outside their room, he assumed it was one of the others. But as the minutes passed, the footsteps didn't fade they circled their door, slow and deliberate.

Saket woke up with a jolt. "What's that?"

Om put a finger to his lips. He motioned toward the door, where the shadow of feet was visible beneath the gap.

Then, as suddenly as it started, the footsteps stopped.

And then, a whisper slithered through the keyhole:

"Are we there yet?"

Om and Saket looked at each other, their bodies rigid with fear. The doorknob rattled violently, as if someone or something was trying to get in.

Then, silence.

Om gathered his courage and tiptoed toward the door. He hesitated before peeking through the peephole.

The hallway was empty.

He let out a shaky breath and turned back toward Saket. But as soon as he stepped away from the door, a faint knock came again.

This time, it came from inside the room.

Downstairs, the receptionist sighed, rubbing his temples as he checked the time. He reached for his phone, hesitating before making a call. His fingers trembled slightly as he dialed a number.

"Sir," he whispered when the call connected. "They're here. The new guests…"

A raspy voice on the other end responded, "Have they heard it yet?"

The receptionist swallowed. "Yes. The whispers have started."

A long silence followed before the voice replied:

"Then it's already too late."

Chapter 7: The Warning

The next morning, the sunlight did little to chase away the unease from the night before. The boys gathered in the hotel's breakfast area, their eyes heavy with lack of sleep. Aryan stirred his coffee absentmindedly, his fingers still trembling from the events in Room 207.

"So…who else had a weird night?" he finally asked.

Saket nearly choked on his toast. "You too?"

Ajay glanced at Ganesh, who nodded slowly. Om remained quiet but gave a knowing look. One by one, they recounted their experiences whispers from the closet, shadowy figures on balconies, footsteps circling their room, and that chilling voice from the keyhole.

"It wasn't a dream," Nikhil murmured. "Something is seriously off about this place."

Aryan's grip tightened around his mug. "We need to find out what's going on."

Ganesh, ever the logical one, leaned forward. "Let's not panic. Maybe there's a rational explanation."

"Rational?" Ajay scoffed. "A ghost in my balcony is 'rational' to you?"

Saket shook his head. "There's something they're not telling us." His eyes flickered toward the receptionist, who was watching them from behind the counter. The man quickly looked away when he noticed Saket's gaze.

Om exhaled sharply. "Then let's ask them."

The group approached the front desk. The receptionist, an older man with sunken eyes, stiffened as they neared.

"Morning, boys," he greeted, forcing a smile. "Sleep well?"

Aryan didn't waste time. "What's wrong with this hotel?"

The man's smile faltered. "I…don't know what you mean."

Saket slammed his hand on the counter. "Don't lie. We all saw and heard things last night."

The receptionist hesitated, glancing around as if making sure no one else was listening. Then, in a hushed voice, he said, "You need to leave."

Om frowned. "What?"

"Check out today. Find another hotel. Don't stay another night."

Nikhil's heart pounded. "Why? What's happening here?"

The receptionist leaned closer. "This hotel... isn't like others. People check in, but some don't check out." His voice dropped lower. "The second floor... it's cursed."

Silence fell over the group. Aryan felt a chill crawl down his spine. "Cursed?"

The man nodded. "Strange noises. Shadows moving. Guests disappearing without a trace. I tried to warn the management, but they don't care. They just keep renting out the rooms."

Ganesh, always the skeptic, crossed his arms. "You expect us to believe that?"

The receptionist sighed. "Believe what you want. But if you hear the whisper again…" He swallowed hard. "Don't answer it."

Ajay's stomach twisted. "And if we already did?"

The man's face paled. He stepped back and whispered, "Then it has already found you."

The boys left the reception area in silence. Fear settled over them like a heavy fog.

"So, what now?" Om asked, breaking the quiet.

"Leaving sounds like a great idea," Aryan muttered.

But Saket shook his head. "No way! We came here to have fun. We're not running because of some spooky stories."

Ajay sighed. "Yeah, plus we already paid for two more nights. That's money down the drain."

Ganesh rubbed his chin, deep in thought. "We stay one more night. But we stick together."

Nikhil exhaled. "And if something happens?"

Om's voice was grim. "Then we make sure we all check out together."

That evening, as the sun began to set, the atmosphere in the hotel changed. The hallways seemed darker, the air heavier. The old wooden floors creaked more than usual. As they walked back to their rooms, they noticed something odd Room 207's door was slightly ajar.

Saket stopped in his tracks. "Didn't we shut that?"

Ajay swallowed hard. "Yeah… we did."

Nikhil took a hesitant step forward. "Maybe the staff came in to clean?"

Ganesh shook his head. "No. That's not how hotels work. Housekeeping knocks first."

Aryan's breath quickened. "So then…who opened it?"

Silence stretched between them. The door creaked wider as if inviting them inside.

Om clenched his fists. "We need to know what's in there."

Saket groaned. "Are you crazy? That's the exact opposite of what we should do."

Ganesh exhaled. "We can't ignore it."

One by one, they stepped inside. The room was eerily still. Their bags were untouched, the beds slightly ruffled from earlier. But then they saw it.

A message scrawled on the mirror in what looked like red ink or was it something else?

YOU SHOULD HAVE LEFT.

Chapter 8: The Hidden Truth

The chilling message on the mirror sent shivers down their spines. Silence engulfed the room as the five friends stared at the red scrawl, their hearts pounding in unison.

Aryan took an involuntary step back. "Nope. Nope. I'm out."

Saket, however, was still brimming with adrenaline. "Alright, who's messing with us?" His voice was laced with forced bravado, but his trembling hands betrayed his fear.

Om carefully approached the mirror and ran a finger over the writing. The red substance smeared slightly. "It's wet…"

Nikhil gulped. "So, someone wrote this just now?"

Ganesh exhaled deeply. "That means someone was in here. While we were downstairs."

Ajay suddenly let out a nervous chuckle. "Alright, guys. Maybe we're overthinking this. Maybe…

Maybe it's some weird prank?" His laughter died when he met the others' serious expressions.

A loud knock on the door made them all jump.

Everyone turned to look at the door, their bodies frozen. The knocking came again three firm, deliberate knocks.

Om took a deep breath and, with shaky hands, opened the door.

The receptionist stood there, his face paler than before. He quickly slipped inside and shut the door behind him. "You saw the message, didn't you?" His voice was a whisper.

Saket narrowed his eyes. "You know something. Tell us."

The man hesitated but then sighed heavily. "This hotel… It has secrets. The second floor, especially Room 207, has a dark past. Decades ago, a guest went missing from this very room. No trace, no evidence just gone."

Aryan's face turned white. "What… what does that have to do with us?"

The receptionist lowered his voice. "Ever since then, strange things happen in this room. Messages appear. Guests hear whispers. Some see shadows. But the worst part?" His voice dropped to a near whisper. "Some guests disappear."

A heavy silence settled over them.

Ganesh, the logical one, pressed further. "If this room is so haunted, why does the hotel still rent it out?"

The receptionist's eyes darted around, checking if anyone was listening. "Because the owner doesn't care. People pay, and if they check out, great. If they disappear, well... no one asks too many questions."

Om clenched his fists. "That's insane. Someone has to have reported this to the police."

The receptionist nodded. "They did. But every time an investigation started, there was no evidence. No proof. Just... vanished guests."

Ajay, who had been silently chewing on his fingernails, finally spoke. "Okay, but we're not disappearing, right? Like, we'll just leave tomorrow morning?"

The receptionist hesitated. "You need to leave tonight."

Nikhil scoffed. "What? Why? What difference does a few hours make?"

The man swallowed hard. "Because the disappearances always happen after the second night." He gave them a meaningful look. "And tonight is your second night."

For a moment, no one spoke. The weight of his words sank in like an anchor in the pit of their stomachs.

Saket, refusing to back down, ran a hand through his hair. "So what do we do? Just run out of here like scared kids?"

The receptionist sighed. "You need to get out before midnight. But whatever you do, don't go alone. Stay together."

A sudden gust of wind made the curtains flutter, even though the windows were shut. The lights flickered.

Aryan grabbed his bag. "I don't need to hear anything else. We're leaving."

Om nodded. "Agreed. Let's get out before it's too late."

Ganesh looked at his watch. It was 10:45 PM.

They had just over an hour to escape.

But something told them it wouldn't be that easy…

As they hastily began packing, the air grew heavier. It felt as if an invisible force was pressing down on them. The dim ceiling light flickered again, casting eerie shadows that seemed to stretch and move on their own.

"Did you hear that?" Nikhil whispered, his eyes darting toward the bathroom.

A faint rustling noise came from within.

Om took a cautious step forward. "We need to check. What if it's another clue?"

Saket shook his head violently. "Or what if it's whatever made those people disappear?"

The doorknob to the bathroom turned.

Everyone held their breath.

With a creaking sound, the door slowly opened on its own, revealing nothing but darkness beyond.

A shiver ran down Ajay's spine. "Screw this, guys. We're leaving. Now."

They grabbed their bags and rushed toward the door. Just as Om reached for the handle, the lights shut off completely, plunging them into darkness.

And then they heard it.

A whisper.

Low. Distorted. Right behind them.

"Stay."

Chapter 9: The Race Against Time

The whisper sent a chill through the group, freezing them in place. Their hearts pounded in unison as they clutched their bags tighter. No one dared to turn around.

Aryan swallowed hard. "Did... did someone just whisper?"

"No, it was the wind!" Ajay said, attempting to convince himself more than anyone else. But his voice trembled.

Ganesh took a deep breath. "Okay, we need to move. Now. Everyone, stay close. We make a run for it."

Om reached for the door handle again, his fingers trembling. The room had grown unbearably cold. As he turned the knob, a sudden force yanked the door shut.

Nikhil screamed. "What the hell was that?!"

The lights flickered back on, but the room felt... different. The walls seemed closer, the shadows darker. The air thickened as if something unseen was watching them.

"This is not normal," Saket muttered. "This place is alive!"

They tried the door again locked. No matter how hard they pushed, it wouldn't budge.

"No, no, no!" Aryan panicked. "The receptionist said we need to leave before midnight. What if we're already trapped?"

Om glanced at his watch 11:10 PM. Fifty minutes left.

Ganesh forced himself to think rationally. "There's got to be another way out. The window!"

They rushed to the window, only to find it sealed shut. Even as they banged on it, it wouldn't crack.

Suddenly, the bathroom door creaked open on its own. A gust of icy air blew out, carrying the faint sound of laughter distorted, unnatural.

"Nope! Not checking that out!" Ajay declared, stepping back.

"We might not have a choice," Om said, his face pale. "If the main door is locked and the windows won't open, there has to be another exit. Maybe a vent, a service door anything."

A sudden knock echoed through the room. But this time, it didn't come from the door. It came from inside the bathroom.

Saket's over excited energy had faded. He was shivering now. "Oh, come on! Who knocks from inside a locked bathroom?!"

The knocking grew louder. More urgent.

Ganesh took a deep breath. "We need to go in. Together."

Om nodded. "Everyone, stay close."

One by one, they stepped toward the bathroom, their shadows stretching unnaturally in the dim light. The knocking stopped. A deafening silence followed.

Om pushed the door open.

The bathroom was empty.

No footprints. No sign of anyone ever being there. Just a foggy mirror and the faint scent of something metallic in the air.

Nikhil noticed a message appearing on the mirror, as if written by an invisible hand:

"Time's almost up."

The clock ticked 11:30 PM. Thirty minutes left.

A loud crash from outside made them all jump. It came from the hallway.

"Forget this! We run for it!" Aryan said, gripping his bag.

"But how? The door's locked!" Nikhil reminded him.

Om clenched his jaw. "Then we break it down. Together."

They braced themselves, counted to three, and hurled their combined weight against the door. It rattled but didn't give way.

Another attempt.

Then another.

The whispers returned. This time, all around them.

"You can't leave."

"Stay."

"Join us."

The lights flickered wildly as an unseen force began pulling them back into the room.

Ajay screamed, "GO!"

With one final push, the door flew open, and they stumbled into the hallway. But what they saw made their blood run cold.

The hallway wasn't the same.

It had changed. Distorted. Stretched impossibly long, as if the hotel itself was shifting.

And at the far end, barely visible in the flickering lights, stood a shadowy figure.

Watching them.

Waiting.

And then, it started moving toward them.

They bolted down the hallway, their footsteps echoing unnaturally. The lights above them flickered, casting eerie, shifting shadows on the walls. The closer they got to the exit sign, the further it seemed to stretch away, as if the hallway had no end.

"This isn't real!" Ganesh shouted. "The hotel is playing with us!"

"We just have to keep running!" Saket gasped, pushing forward.

Suddenly, the walls shifted again. Doors lining the hallway swung open violently, revealing empty, dark rooms. A forceful gust of wind howled through, almost knocking them off their feet.

"Don't stop!" Om yelled.

As they ran, the shadowy figure behind them picked up speed, its footsteps eerily silent. The closer it got, the more the air around them grew heavy, like an unseen weight pressing down on their chests.

Aryan glanced back. "It's gaining on us!"

Nikhil spotted something ahead a stairwell door, slightly ajar. "There!"

With one final push, they lunged toward it, yanking it open just as the shadow lunged. They tumbled inside, slamming the door shut.

Silence.

No whispers.

No footsteps.

Just their own heavy breathing.

Ajay collapsed against the wall. "Okay... someone tell me this is all a dream."

"If it is, we all had the same one," Om muttered.

Ganesh checked his watch. 11:45 PM.

Fifteen minutes left.

Nikhil peered through the small window on the door. The hallway outside had returned to normal.

"Do we go back out?" Saket whispered.

"I don't think we have a choice," Om said. "The exit is somewhere ahead. We just have to make it before midnight."

Gathering their courage, they stepped out of the stairwell.

The hallway was quiet now. Too quiet.

And then, from behind them, a slow, rhythmic knock.

It wasn't over yet.

Chapter 10: The Midnight Escape

The knock behind them sent a shiver down their spines. It was slow, deliberate, as if whatever was on the other side knew they were trapped.

Aryan clenched his fists. "No. Nope. We are not dealing with this again!"

Ganesh checked his watch. **11:50 PM.** "We have ten minutes. We need to find the exit now!"

Om took a deep breath, his mind racing. "Okay, let's think. The exit should be ahead, but if the hotel keeps shifting, it might not be where it's supposed to be. We need to move fast and stay together."

Ajay gulped. "You know what? I think we should just stay here and accept our fate."

Saket grabbed Ajay's wrist. "Over my dead body! Move!"

As they rushed down the corridor, the air thickened again, the walls seeming to pulsate as if alive. The lights above them flickered erratically, casting eerie, stretching shadows that danced on the walls.

A distorted voice echoed from behind. "Don't go… stay…"

Aryan's breath hitched. "I don't know about you guys, but I'm gonna run like hell."

They sprinted, the distant exit sign glowing dimly in the darkness. But with each step they took, the corridor seemed to extend, the door pushing further away.

"No, no, no!" Nikhil yelled. "This isn't possible!"

Suddenly, the walls cracked, revealing glimpses of another dimension a void of swirling black mist and shadowy figures. Whispering voices filled the air, pleading, crying, *laughing*.

Ganesh grabbed Om's arm. "It's an illusion! The hotel is trying to break us. Don't stop running!"

A piercing scream erupted behind them. Ajay dared to glance back and instantly regretted it. The shadowy figure was no longer just a shape it had eyes. Hollow, glowing, and locked onto them.

"RUN!" he screamed.

With renewed adrenaline, they surged forward. The walls trembled violently, the hotel groaning as if resisting their escape. The floor beneath them shifted, parts of it vanishing into darkness.

"Jump!" Saket shouted as he leaped over a sudden gap in the floor.

Each of them barely made it across, their feet skidding on the unstable ground. The exit door was just a few meters away now, but the shadowy figure was closing in, moving unnaturally fast.

"GO GO GO!" Om yelled.

Ganesh reached the door first, shoving it open. A blast of cold air hit them as they tumbled outside into the parking lot. The second they crossed the threshold, the heavy silence returned. No whispers. No shadows.

They turned around the hotel was back to normal. The windows still, the walls intact. The haunting presence gone.

Nikhil checked his phone. **12:01 AM.**

"We made it," Saket whispered, his voice barely audible.

Aryan collapsed onto the pavement. "I swear, I am never booking a cheap hotel again!"

Om panted, still staring at the building. "Was it real? Or did we just imagine all of that?"

Ganesh looked down at his arms dark handprints stained his shirt. "It was real. And we got lucky."

Ajay exhaled heavily. "I need food. Right now. I don't care if the kitchen is haunted too. I need food."

They all laughed shaky, relieved laughter.

But as they turned away from the hotel, none of them noticed the small, shadowy figure watching them from the top floor window.

Smiling.

Just as they began catching their breath, a gust of wind howled through the parking lot. The car alarm of their vehicle blared suddenly, flashing its headlights in a chaotic rhythm.

"Oh, come on! Not the car too!" Aryan groaned.

Om cautiously stepped toward it, but as soon as he touched the door handle, the alarm stopped. Everything went dead silent again.

Nikhil was still shaking. "Guys… this place is cursed. I swear, the sooner we get out of here, the better."

Ganesh scanned the lot. "The hotel let us go, but it feels like it's still watching us."

Saket turned to Om. "Dude, start the car. Now."

Om nodded and quickly unlocked the car. They all piled in, slamming the doors shut. He turned the key in the ignition nothing. The engine was completely dead.

"Oh, fantastic!" Ajay groaned, slamming his head against the seat. "Guess we're spending the night here after all."

"Shut up!" Aryan snapped. "We need a new plan. Fast."

Saket pulled out his phone, his hands trembling. "No signal."

Ganesh clenched his jaw. "We should have known. The hotel isn't going to let us go that easily."

Om gripped the steering wheel. "Alright, everyone stay calm. We'll figure this out."

A slow, deliberate knock echoed from the trunk.

Silence.

Their breaths hitched as they turned in unison. The knocking came again louder this time.

Ajay's voice wavered. "P please tell me we didn't pick up a hitchhiker…"

Saket swallowed hard. "Guys… we have two options. One we open it and see what's inside. Two we run."

Aryan shook his head violently. "I pick option three scream and faint."

Ganesh took a deep breath. "We have to face it. On three…"

"One…"

"Two…"

Om popped the trunk.

It was empty.

Nothing. Just their luggage, untouched. But as they stood there, confused, a whisper drifted through the night.

"See you soon…"

And then, the car engine roared to life by itself.

No one moved.

"Drive. Drive. DRIVE!" Nikhil screamed.

Om slammed the door shut, shifted into gear, and floored the accelerator. The car screeched as it sped out of the parking lot, the haunted hotel disappearing in the rearview mirror.

But deep inside, each of them knew this wasn't over.

Not yet.

Chapter 11: The Aftermath

The car tore down the highway, headlights slicing through the dense fog that had crept in from the coastline. No one spoke. The only sound was the hum of the engine and the occasional nervous breath. The haunting events at the hotel had shaken them all to their core.

Om tightened his grip on the steering wheel, glancing at the rearview mirror every few seconds, as if expecting to see something chasing them.

"Where are we even going?" Aryan finally asked, breaking the silence.

"Anywhere but there," Nikhil muttered, staring out the window. "We just need distance."

Ajay slumped in his seat. "I don't even care if we sleep in the car at this point. Just as long as I can get some food first."

Saket, who had been oddly quiet, suddenly burst out laughing. It was a strange, nervous laugh. "I mean, come on! What the hell was that? Did we just survive a haunted hotel? Are we in a horror movie?!"

Ganesh sighed. "Honestly? It felt like it. But there has to be a logical explanation. Maybe we were hallucinating. Maybe the air had something weird in it. Maybe "

"Maybe we should stop talking about it," Om interjected, his voice firm. "We're safe now. Let's just focus on finding a place to rest."

The highway stretched ahead, an endless ribbon of darkness. After half an hour, they finally spotted a roadside dhaba, its neon sign flickering in the night. It looked normal, welcoming even.

"Food! Finally!" Ajay cheered as he leaped out of the car before it even came to a full stop.

The others followed, exhaustion weighing them down. As they stepped inside, the warm aroma of spices and freshly cooked parathas filled the air, instantly lifting their spirits. The place was empty except for an old man sitting at the counter, lazily flipping through a newspaper.

"Welcome, welcome!" he greeted them, barely looking up. "What will you have?"

"Everything," Ajay replied without hesitation.

As they sat at a table, waiting for their order, Saket nudged Ganesh. "Hey… do you think we should tell someone about what happened? I mean, what if other people end up in that hotel?"

Ganesh hesitated, then shook his head. "Who would believe us? And besides… we made it out. Let's just be grateful for that."

Nikhil glanced at the old man at the counter, then back at Ganesh. "Or… we could ask if he knows anything about that place? Maybe there's a history behind it."

Om leaned back. "I'd rather forget about it. But… I admit, I'm curious too."

As they debated, their food arrived piping hot and smelling heavenly. They dug in, momentarily distracted from their ordeal.

But just as they were finishing, the old man spoke up, his voice eerily calm. "You boys… came from that old hotel, didn't you?"

Silence.

Their stomachs twisted. Ajay nearly choked on his last bite.

"How do you know?" Aryan asked cautiously.

The old man sighed, setting down his newspaper. "Because… no one ever comes from that road at this hour. And those who do… don't usually look as shaken as you lot."

A cold shiver ran through them.

"So… you do know something?" Nikhil pressed.

The old man nodded. "That place… it wasn't always haunted. But years ago, something happened there. Something terrible. And ever since then, it's been cursed."

Ajay swallowed hard. "What kind of… something?"

The old man hesitated. "A group of travelers. Just like you. They checked in… but never checked out.

No bodies were ever found. Only their belongings, neatly packed, as if they had never been there at all."

Saket paled. "And no one investigated?"

"They did," the old man said. "But the hotel was empty. No staff. No guests. Just an abandoned building that… sometimes… isn't so abandoned."

The boys exchanged uneasy glances.

Ganesh exhaled sharply. "Okay. That's enough ghost stories for one night. Let's just pay the bill and get out of here."

But as Om reached for his wallet, his hands froze. Inside, tucked among his cash, was a folded note.

A note that none of them had put there.

With shaky fingers, he unfolded it. One sentence was scrawled in red ink:

"You never really left."

The blood drained from Om's face.

"Guys… I think we have a problem."

A gust of wind howled outside, rattling the old wooden windows of the dhaba. The neon light above the entrance flickered violently before going out completely, plunging the place into dim candlelight. The old man's face, partially illuminated by the wavering flames, seemed to harden with an unreadable expression.

"I was hoping you'd be just another bunch of tourists," he muttered under his breath. "But it looks like... it has chosen you."

"What the hell does that mean?" Nikhil snapped, his voice shaking.

The old man ignored the question and stood up, moving toward a wooden chest in the corner. With a deep breath, he unlocked it, revealing an assortment of old newspaper clippings, rusted keys, and a single, dust covered book with a leather binding. He slid it across the table to them.

"Read it," he said. "And pray that you find the answer before it's too late."

Aryan, hands trembling, picked up the book and wiped off the dust. The title, barely visible, sent a fresh wave of fear through them all.

The Cursed Hotel: The Lost Souls That Never Returned.

The pages rustled as he opened it, and the first words made his heart pound:

The guests who leave... never really leave.

A low creak echoed through the dhaba, as if something or someone had just stepped inside.

"Guys..." Om whispered, eyes wide. "We are not alone."

Chapter 12: The Unfinished Story

A thick silence settled over the dhaba, heavy and suffocating. The dim candlelight cast eerie shadows on the walls, flickering wildly as if disturbed by an unseen presence. The old man's words still lingered in the air, sending a chill down each of their spines.

Om gripped the book tightly, his hands shaking. "What do you mean, 'never really leave'?"

The old man sighed, his weathered face unreadable. "That hotel… it has a way of holding on to its guests. Some say it's cursed, others say it's a doorway to something beyond our world. Those who enter never leave the same. And some… never leave at all."

Saket, still trying to keep his nerves in check, let out a nervous chuckle. "Alright, old man, great story. But we got out, right? So whatever that curse is, it didn't work on us."

The old man leaned in, his dark eyes glinting under the dim light. "Are you sure about that?"

A gust of wind howled outside, rattling the wooden windows. The neon sign above the entrance flickered once, then died completely, plunging them into near darkness. Ajay instinctively reached for his phone, but his screen refused to turn on.

"Uh, guys…" Ajay's voice wavered. "I think my phone is dead."

One by one, the others checked their phones. Nothing. All were drained, as if something had sucked the life out of them.

"Okay, this is getting way too creepy," Aryan muttered, his anxiety rising. "Let's just get out of here. We can deal with this in the morning."

Ganesh nodded. "Agreed. We'll find another place to stay and put this whole nightmare behind us."

The old man didn't stop them as they rose from their seats. He simply sat back, watching them with a knowing look. "Remember," he called out as they made their way to the door, "the story isn't over yet."

Ignoring him, they hurried to their car. Om fumbled with the keys, but just as he was about to start the engine, something caught his eye in the rearview mirror.

A figure. Standing at the edge of the dhaba's parking lot.

It was barely visible in the darkness, but the silhouette was unmistakable.

A tall man in a black coat, his head tilted slightly, as if observing them.

"Did you guys see that?" Om whispered, his grip tightening on the steering wheel.

"See what?" Nikhil asked, glancing around. "What are you talking about?"

Om swallowed hard. The figure was gone.

He hesitated for a moment before shaking his head. "Nothing… just my imagination. Let's go."

The engine roared to life, and they sped away from the dhaba, desperate to leave behind the nightmarish events that had unfolded.

But as they drove, a dreadful realization crept over them.

No matter how far they went, the road stretched endlessly ahead, looping back into the same dark highway.

And the neon sign of the dhaba flickered back to life in their rearview mirror.

They had never left.

A sudden static noise filled the car's radio, though none of them had touched it. The voices whispering through the interference were faint but chillingly familiar.

"You shouldn't have left... you shouldn't have left..."

Saket turned the volume knob frantically, but the whispers only grew louder. "Guys, what the hell is going on?" His voice cracked as the words became clearer.

"Turn around. Come back. Finish the story."

Om slammed his foot on the brake, the tires screeching against the asphalt. The car shuddered to a halt, and for a moment, silence reigned. Then, without warning, the car doors unlocked with a loud *click* on their own.

"Nope! Nope! Nope!" Ajay shouted, frantically trying to relock them. "This is some horror movie crap, and I am NOT starring in it!"

Ganesh's face was pale as he whispered, "We were never supposed to leave. That place... that hotel. It's still with us."

Nikhil wiped the sweat from his forehead. "We have to go back, don't we?" he asked, his voice barely above a whisper.

Aryan, trembling, slowly nodded. "If we don't... we may never escape."

Reluctantly, Om turned the car around. As they drove back towards the dhaba, a thick fog rolled in, swallowing the road behind them. The world outside seemed to blur, the night distorting into something unreal.

And then, as they reached the parking lot, they saw it.

The hotel.

Standing exactly where the dhaba had been just moments ago.

The doors were open.

And inside, the dim lights flickered in eerie welcome.

Chapter 13: The Hotel's Secret

The car came to a screeching halt just outside the entrance of the hotel. The neon sign above the door flickered ominously, now displaying a name they hadn't noticed before: *The Eternal Stay Inn.*

Om's hands were still gripping the steering wheel tightly, his knuckles turning white. "This isn't happening… This isn't real."

"Oh, it's real, alright!" Saket shouted, his usual excitement replaced with panic. "That dhaba just turned into a hotel! How the hell does that even happen?!"

Ganesh, always the logical one, took a deep breath. "We have two choices. Drive into the fog and risk getting lost in some endless loop or go inside and figure out what's going on."

Aryan rubbed his temples, already feeling a headache forming. "I hate both those choices."

"Yeah? Well, guess what? We don't have a third one!" Ajay grumbled. "And I'm starving. Maybe this cursed hotel has a kitchen."

Nikhil, the only one who still had a hint of curiosity left, unbuckled his seatbelt. "We have to go inside. We need answers."

With hesitant steps, they approached the hotel doors, which creaked open as if welcoming them. The lobby was grand, much larger than it appeared from the outside. A massive chandelier hung from the ceiling, casting eerie shadows on the walls. The air smelled faintly of old wood and something else… something rotten.

Behind the reception desk stood a tall, gaunt man in an outdated uniform. His pale face was devoid of expression, and his deep set eyes followed their every move.

"Welcome back," he said in a slow, deliberate tone.

A cold shiver ran down Om's spine. "Back? We've never been here before."

The receptionist's thin lips curled into something that resembled a smile. "Haven't you?"

Silence hung in the air. The group exchanged uneasy glances before Ganesh stepped forward. "Listen, we just want to know what's happening. We were at a dhaba, and suddenly, we're back here. What is this place?"

The receptionist reached beneath the desk and pulled out a large, leather bound register. He flipped through the pages, finally stopping at one and turning the book toward them. Their eyes widened in horror.

Written in ink, in their own handwriting, were their names.

And next to them… check in dates.

But no check out dates.

"No. No, no, no!" Saket stammered. "This has to be a prank. There's no way we've been here before!"

The receptionist simply nodded toward the grand staircase leading to the upper floors. "Your rooms are ready."

Aryan grabbed Om's arm. "We should leave. Now."

Om took a shaky breath. "We already tried that. What if leaving isn't an option?"

Ajay, despite his fear, found himself asking, "What if… we really have been here before?"

The question sent a fresh wave of dread through them.

Nikhil gulped. "Then the real question is… why don't we remember?"

Suddenly, a sharp gust of wind howled through the lobby, causing the chandelier to sway. The lights flickered, and for a brief second, the reflection in the lobby mirror did not match their movements. Aryan turned to point it out, but before he could speak, the receptionist's voice cut through the silence.

"The night is still young, gentlemen. You should get some rest."

"Rest?!" Saket scoffed. "In a haunted hotel? No, thanks!"

But before anyone could protest further, a loud chime echoed through the hotel. The old grandfather clock in the corner struck midnight. At that precise moment, the doors behind them slammed shut with a deafening bang.

Ajay jumped. "Nope. Nope. This is some horror movie nonsense. We're getting out of here."

He rushed toward the door and yanked at the handle, but it wouldn't budge. No matter how hard he pulled, the heavy wooden doors refused to move. He turned back to the group, his face pale. "Guys… we're trapped."

A deep, unsettling chuckle rumbled from the receptionist. "Welcome home."

Chapter 14: The Unfinished Business

A deafening silence followed the receptionist's ominous words. The six friends stood frozen, their minds struggling to grasp the gravity of their situation. The doors behind them remained sealed shut, trapping them inside *The Eternal Stay Inn.*

"Welcome home?" Aryan repeated, his voice barely above a whisper. "What the hell does that mean?!"

Om swallowed hard, his gaze darting around the dimly lit lobby. "We need to stay calm. There has to be a way out."

"Forget staying calm!" Saket burst out. "That creepy dude just said 'welcome home' like we've been here before! What if we " he hesitated, lowering his voice. "What if we never left?"

A shiver ran down Nikhil's spine. "No. That's ridiculous. We were just on the road. We were at the dhaba. We drove here. There's no way "

"Then how do you explain this?" Ganesh interrupted, tapping the guest register. Their names glared back at them in dark ink, paired with check in dates that made no sense. They had no memory of signing anything, let alone staying here.

Ajay, ever the skeptic, let out a nervous chuckle. "Maybe this is some elaborate prank? Hidden cameras? A weird social experiment?"

"Yeah, because 'trapping six guys in a haunted hotel' is totally a normal prank," Aryan muttered. He turned toward the receptionist. "Look, we don't know what kind of game this is, but we want out. Now."

The receptionist merely tilted his head, his hollow gaze unreadable. "There is no game. You have unfinished business here."

A loud *boom* echoed through the hotel as the chandelier rattled above them. Dust rained down from the ceiling, and a gust of wind rushed through the lobby, extinguishing several of the wall mounted lamps. Shadows danced along the walls, stretching unnaturally.

"What was that?!" Saket yelped, grabbing Om's arm.

Ganesh squared his shoulders. "Alright, enough with the cryptic nonsense. What unfinished business? We don't remember ever being here."

"That is because the past does not reveal itself so easily," the receptionist said, turning the book toward them again. This time, something had changed. The ink on the pages shifted and twisted, forming words they hadn't seen before.

A life left behind. A debt unpaid. A truth forgotten.

Aryan took a shaky step back. "This place is messing with our heads."

"Or," Nikhil whispered, his eyes scanning the words again, "it's trying to remind us of something."

Suddenly, a door creaked open at the far end of the lobby. A narrow hallway stretched beyond it, the flickering lanterns casting eerie shadows along its length.

"Great," Ajay mumbled. "Because *that* doesn't scream 'bad idea.'"

Om exhaled deeply. "We don't have much of a choice. If we want answers, we need to go in."

Saket groaned. "Horror movie rule #1: Never go toward the creepy hallway."

Ganesh smirked. "And yet, here we are."

Reluctantly, the group stepped forward, their footsteps echoing eerily as they entered the corridor. The air grew heavier with each step, and the walls seemed to close in slightly. The lamps flickered erratically, revealing faded portraits on the walls. The faces in the paintings bore unsettling resemblances to… them.

Ajay stopped in his tracks. "Tell me I'm imagining this."

Om's voice was barely audible. "No… I see it too."

They were looking at six portraits, each one labeled with a name. Their names. But beneath them were dates they didn't recognize. Some from years ago.

Aryan's breath hitched. "Why are there death dates under our names?"

Before anyone could answer, the hallway trembled, and a chilling whisper echoed around them.

"Find the truth… before the truth finds you."

As the whisper faded, the walls around them seemed to shift, elongating unnaturally. The floor groaned beneath their feet, as if something ancient and unseen stirred below. The portraits flickered like mirages, revealing glimpses of the figures within moving watching them.

Saket clutched his chest. "Okay, no. Nope. I'm out. We need to "

His words were cut off by a sudden gust of wind that howled through the corridor, slamming the door shut behind them. The sound reverberated like a final warning.

"We're locked in," Nikhil muttered. "Again."

Ganesh approached one of the portraits, tracing the eerie resemblance of his own face with a hesitant finger. The moment he touched it, the image shimmered and transformed. Now, it wasn't just him it was all six of them, standing in the very corridor they were in. And behind them, a shadowy figure loomed.

"Guys..." Ganesh whispered, stepping back. "Something's behind us."

Slowly, they turned. The lanterns dimmed, casting deep, crawling shadows across the floor. And at the far end of the hallway, barely visible in the darkness, stood a figure. Its presence was more felt than seen an overwhelming weight pressing against their chests, making it harder to breathe.

Then, it moved.

A low, raspy voice drifted through the air. "You came back... just like you promised."

A cold realization settled in. Whatever this was, it knew them. It had been waiting.

And it was not alone.

Chapter 15: The Final Truth

The hallway seemed to stretch endlessly as the shadowy figure advanced toward them. The lanterns flickered violently, casting grotesque silhouettes on the walls. The air was thick with an unshakable sense of déjà vu, as if they had all been here before trapped in this moment, repeating a cycle they didn't understand.

"What do you mean, we came back?" Om asked, his voice steady despite the fear gripping him.

The figure's hollow eyes locked onto them. "You made a promise... long ago. And now, it is time to fulfill it."

A chilling breeze swept through the corridor, making Aryan shudder. "This is insane! We've never been here before!" He turned toward the others. "Right?"

Ganesh stared at the ghostly portraits lining the walls, their faces shifting as though whispering secrets of the past. "I don't know anymore. But if there's a truth we're missing, we need to find it."

Saket groaned. "I hate this. I hate this so much. Can't we just wake up from this nightmare already?"

"What if it's not a nightmare?" Nikhil whispered. "What if this is real? What if… we were meant to be here?"

Ajay, who had been unusually quiet, suddenly spoke. "What if we *never left*?"

His words sent a shockwave through the group. The silence that followed was deafening.

The figure extended an ashen hand, pointing toward an old wooden door at the end of the corridor. "The truth lies beyond. If you wish to leave, you must remember."

They exchanged uncertain glances, but there was no turning back now. Ganesh took the lead, pushing open the creaking door. Inside was a massive, dust covered ballroom. Chandeliers dangled precariously from the ceiling, their crystals dulled by time. A long dining table stretched across the room, set for a feast that had long since rotted away.

But the worst part wasn't the eerie setting it was the six chairs at the table. Each had a name engraved on its back.

Their names.

"Okay, this is officially the creepiest thing I've ever seen," Saket muttered.

Nikhil approached one of the chairs hesitantly, running his fingers over his own name. "This doesn't make sense…"

Then, without warning, the chandeliers burst to life, bathing the room in a golden glow. The walls shimmered, and in an instant, the entire ballroom transformed. The decay was gone, replaced by grandeur. The table was adorned with fresh food, the air filled with the hum of music and laughter.

Ghostly figures materialized, dressed in elegant attire. The six friends gasped as they watched versions of themselves identical in appearance seated at the table, laughing, drinking, celebrating.

"What… is this?" Aryan stammered.

The shadowy figure's voice drifted through the air. "A memory. The night it all began."

Ganesh's breath hitched. "Began? What began?"

The room darkened once more, the joyous scene shifting to chaos. The ghostly versions of themselves were no longer celebrating. They were shouting, arguing. Glass shattered, and suddenly, an ear piercing scream rang out.

Then darkness.

When the light returned, the six figures at the table had slumped over, lifeless. Their drinks spilled, their faces frozen in horror.

Aryan clutched his head. "No. No, this can't be real."

"We... we died?" Nikhil whispered.

The figure stepped closer, its form shifting, revealing a pale, skeletal face. "You made a pact that night. To always return. To always remember. But you never did. Until now."

Ajay took a step back. "That's impossible. We're alive. We've been living our lives!"

"Or so you believed," the figure murmured. "This place exists beyond time, beyond life and death. Each time you return, you forget. And each time, you must remember... before the cycle begins again."

The realization was crushing. This wasn't just a haunted hotel it was a prison, a loop they had been stuck in for who knew how long.

"Then how do we break it?" Ganesh asked, his fists clenched. "How do we stop this?"

The figure gestured toward the table. "Sit. Face what you have done. Only then can the cycle be broken."

A dreadful silence filled the air. One by one, they hesitated before reluctantly taking their places. As they did, flashes of the past returned memories they had buried deep. The fight, the betrayal, the terrible accident that had sealed their fate.

Tears welled in Aryan's eyes. "We did this... to ourselves."

The figure nodded. "Now… let go."

A bright light engulfed the room, and a powerful force pulled them backward. It was like being sucked through time itself, memories unraveling, reality distorting

Then

They awoke.

The morning sun streamed through the hotel windows. The six friends sat in their car, parked in front of *The Eternal Stay Inn*.

"Guys…?" Om's voice trembled. "Are we… alive?"

Saket patted himself down. "I think so?"

Ganesh turned to the hotel. It looked normal no eerie shadows, no ghostly figures. Just a regular building under the bright morning sky.

"Was it all… a dream?" Nikhil asked.

Aryan exhaled shakily. "Maybe. Or maybe it was a warning."

Ajay, looking uncharacteristically serious, whispered, "Let's just leave. Now."

No one argued. They started the car and drove away, the hotel growing smaller in the rearview mirror. None of them spoke for a long time.

Then, just as they reached the outskirts of Goa, Saket let out a nervous laugh. "Well… that was *one* hell of a trip."

The tension broke, and suddenly, they were laughing hysterically, uncontrollably. Maybe it was relief, maybe it was lingering fear. But one thing was certain.

They were never coming back.

As they disappeared down the road, a shadow flickered across the *Vacancy* sign outside *The Eternal Stay Inn.*

And for a brief moment, the words shimmered.

'See you again soon.'

Acknowledgments

Writing this book has been an incredible journey, much like the adventure within its pages. I want to extend my heartfelt gratitude to everyone who supported me along the way.

A special thanks to my friends, whose crazy ideas and unforgettable trips inspired many moments in this story. To my family, for their constant encouragement. And to you, the readerthank you for picking up this book and embarking on this thrilling journey with me.

Other Books by Ajay Chavan

The Forgotten Diary : Breaking The Cycle

About the Author

Ajay Chavan is a passionate writer specializing in mystery, suspense, and thriller novels. With a deep fascination for psychological intrigue and the unknown, Ajay weaves stories that leave readers questioning reality.
Follow Ajay on Instagram: @ajaychavan9910